ALWAYS BE A Unicorn

Story by Pearl E. Horne | Illustrations by Kendra Spanjer

BAILIWICK PRESS

Published by: BAILIWICK PRESS • 309 East Mulberry Street, Fort Collins, Colorado 80524 • www.bailiwickpress.com • ISBN 978-1-934649-79-4

Printed in Canada

You are a unicorn.

Oh, yes you are.

You're magical. REMARKABLE!
A once-in-infinity miracle.

So hold that horn high! And be confidently, majestically YOU.

But **whoa there** a swaggering second.

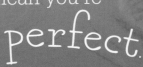

Just because you're a unicorn doesn't mean you're **perfect**.

When you mess up, which happens sometimes, even to unicorns...

...say you're sorry, put things right, and sparkle on.

And if ever you're lost?

Just send up a signal. Noble helpers wait in the wings.

You are beloved, and you are *believed* in.

That's why a group of unicorns is called a

And yep, you're right.
Unicorns come in **all** shapes and sizes.

Because actually, it's not what's on the
outside that makes you a unicorn...
it's what's on the **inside**

Like courage. And wisdom. And grace. And most of all,

deepest-
down
goodness.

Which means, of course

...that **anyone** can be a unicorn!

Yes, you. AND YOU. And YOU.

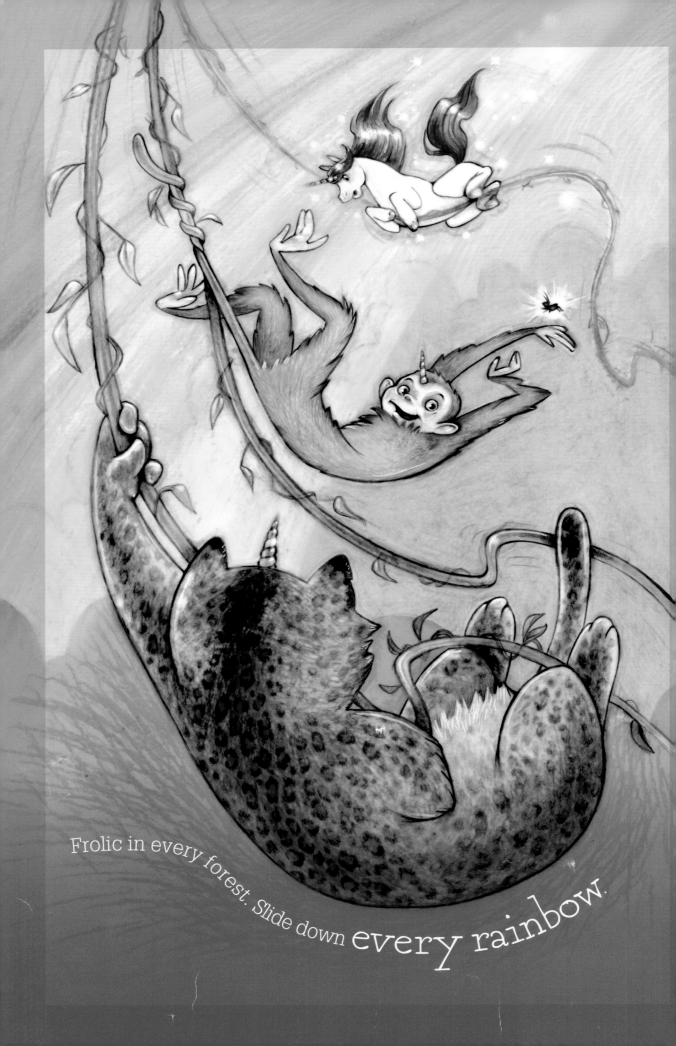

Frolic in every forest. Slide down every rainbow.

Swim in every glittery sea.
And whenever you get the chance...

...FLY!

Whatever fills you with true joy, do that.
Let your unicorn instincts guide you.

Keep close with your crew, no matter how motley.

And the trolls? Treat them with kindness.

For they're miserable enough already. Whenever you can, take the high road.

Be pure of heart and fleet of foot.

And charge fearlessly in the direction of your most

outlandish dreams.

Because time is short, and they're not just any dreams—
they're **unicorn dreams**.

(They're why you're here.)

You see, before you were born,

your unicorn-ness was written in the stars.

So shine *ever-so brightly*

And always, ALWAYS, always
be the unicorn you are.